Ted in a red bed

Russell Punter
Adapted from a story by Phil Roxbee Cox
Illustrated by Stephen Cartwright

Designed by Hope Reynolds
Edited by Jenny Tyler and Lesley Sims
Reading consultants: Alison Kelly and Anne Washtell

There is a little yellow duck to find on every page.

Ted is out on a shopping spree.

"Just what I need," he shouts.

"That red bed's grand,"
he says with a grin.

Ted grabs his bag and heads on in.

Ted tries the bed before he buys.

He snuggles up. "Yes, just my size."

But he's so snug, he falls asleep.

"We'll take him home,"
say Penguin's team.

Penguin helps them with the plan.

"Quick, carry Ted into my van!"

They take Ted home.
He starts to sigh.

In his dream,
the bed flies high.

They set Ted down.

Soon, Ted yawns and looks around.

"I'm home!" says Ted.

He gives a cry...

"It seems my bed can really fly!"

Puzzles

Puzzle 1

What is Ted doing?
Match the words to
the pictures.

jumping
dreaming
walking

A

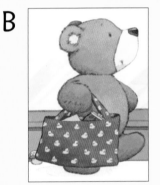

B

C

Puzzle 2

One word is wrong in this speech bubble.
What should it say?

Puzzle 3
Spot the six differences between the two pictures.

Puzzle 4
Choose the right speech bubble for the picture.

Answers to puzzles

Puzzle 1

A

dreaming

B

walking

C

jumping

Puzzle 2

Don't <u>make</u> a sound!

Puzzle 3

Puzzle 4

This bed is cheap!

About phonics

Phonics is a method of teaching reading used extensively in today's schools. At its heart is an emphasis on identifying the *sounds* of letters, or combinations of letters, that are then put together to make words. These sounds are known as phonemes.

Starting to read

Learning to read is an important milestone for any child. The process can begin well before children start to learn letters and put them together to read words. The sooner children can discover books and enjoy stories and language, the better they will be prepared for reading themselves, first with the help of an adult and then independently.

You can find out more about phonics on the Usborne Very First Reading website, **Usborne.com/veryfirstreading** (US readers go to **www.veryfirstreading.com**). Click on the **Parents** tab at the top of the page, then scroll down and click on **About synthetic phonics**.

Phonemic awareness

An important early stage in pre-reading and early reading is developing phonemic awareness: that is, listening out for the sounds within words. Rhymes, rhyming stories and alliteration are excellent ways of encouraging phonemic awareness.

In this story, your child will soon identify the *e* sound, as in **red** and **bed**. Look out, too, for rhymes such as **team** – **dream** and **sigh** – **high**.

Hearing your child read

If your child is reading a story to you, don't rush to correct mistakes, but be ready to prompt or guide if he or she is struggling. Above all, give plenty of praise and encouragement.